Miss Lina's Ballerinas

and the

Prince

XZ
M

By Grace Maccarone

Illustrated by Christine Davenier

FEIWEL AND FRIENDS

New York

To Suzanne Weyn, adventurous spirit and longtime friend,
for giving me the courage to extend my boundaries—G. M.

Pour Louis Bourjac, mon prince!—C. D.

Acknowledgments

I thank Diana Ranola, Dieter Riesle, Eric Hu, Maralyn Miles, Mike Young, and Vicky Sturner for sharing their experiences, insights, and expertise—and most of all, their love of dance. I am grateful to Christine Davenier, for bringing the ballerinas to life. They are perfect! And thanks to Jean Feiwel, Liz Szabla, Holly West, Elizabeth Tardiff, Rich Deas, Gabby Oravetz, and the enthusiastic Macmillan publicity, marketing, and sales teams.—G.M.

A FEIWEL AND FRIENDS BOOK
An Imprint of Macmillan

Library of Congress Cataloging-in-Publication Data Available

ISBN: 978-0-312-64963-0

Book design by Elizabeth Tardiff

Feiwel and Friends logo designed by Filomena Tuosto

First Edition: 2011

10 9 8 7 6 5 4 3 2 1

mackids.com

NOV 2 8 2011

In a cozy white house, in the town of Messina,
nine little girls studied dance with Miss Lina.

Christina, Edwina, Sabrina, Justina,
Katrina, Bettina, Marina, Regina,

and Nina took classes.

And when they were done,
they went to the zoo,
where they danced just for fun.

Then one sunny day, as class came to a close,
Miss Lina, while taking a classical pose,

announced to the girls, in her elegant way,
a dancer would join them the following day.

"He's a boy," said Miss Lina. "I want you to know.
He will join us for class and our end-of-year show."

The girls were delighted, the girls were aglow.
They would dance with a boy in their end-of-year show.

The girls each thought, "Oh!
When I dance with the boy, how exquisite I'll be.
The audience, of course, will be looking at me!"

To dance with a prince in her first *pas de deux*
would be very special, each one of them knew.

When nine ballerinas were snug in their beds,
pas de deux visions danced in their heads.

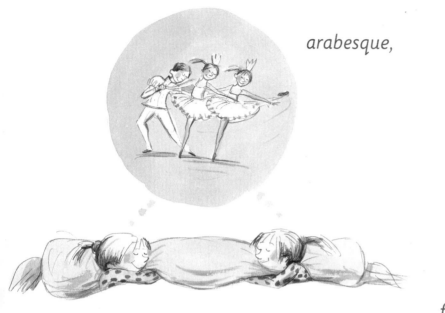

arabesque,

fondue,

développé,

penché,

He looked all around him, feeling quite shy
to see so much pink and be only one guy.

pirouette,

attitude,

promenade,

fouetté.

While nine ballerinas took class the next day,
the weather outside became cloudy and gray.
There was thunder and lightning, it started to pour.

Then a boy, drenched and dripping,
walked in through the door.

Miss Lina said, "Nina, Christina, Edwina,
Sabrina, Justina, Katrina, Bettina,
Marina, Regina, meet Tony Farina."

Dancing with girls was not at all fun.
Quick as a flash, he started to run . . .

and he jumped and he leaped, beat his feet, then he spun.

He took a short rest, but he wasn't quite done.

He took three big steps, then he bounced off the floor,
did a split in the air, and he soared out the door!

The girls were astounded, bewildered, amazed,
stupefied, startled, dazzled, and dazed.

"*Chassé*," said Miss Lina.
"Get him. Now GO!"

But nine ballerinas crossed arms and said, "No!
We don't want that show-off in our end-of-year show."

Then Miss Lina replied in her elegant way,

saying, "I know what's best, dears. You should obey."

Spinning and skipping, and pointing their feet,
nine ballerinas ran out to the street.

They danced to the park.

They danced to the zoo.

And soon they discovered, the boy was there, too.

He lunged like a lion, he kicked like a donkey,

he dove like a dolphin,

and sprung like a monkey.

The nine ballerinas agreed, "He can dance.
Though he's not quite a prince, we can give him a chance."
Then one dancing boy and nine ballerinas
galloped like ponies back to Miss Lina's.

The girls soon found out they could really enjoy
dancing in class with a non-princely boy.

Together they sprung and they lunged and they spun.
By and by, the boy learned *pas de deux* could be fun.

At the end-of-year show, nine lithe ballerinas

and one lively boy danced their best for Miss Lina.

When the dancing was over, the audience clapped loudly;
Christina, Edwina, Sabrina, Justina,
Katrina, Bettina, Marina, Regina,
and Nina, and finally Tony Farina—
Miss Lina's ten dancers—all took their bows proudly.

Ballet Terms

arabesque

(a-ra-BESK)

one leg straight back

attitude

(a-ti-TOOD)

one leg bent

chassé

(shah-SAY)

chase

développé

(duh-veh-luh-PAY)

working foot to standing knee,
then straight out

fondue

(fahn-DOO)

on one bent leg

fouetté

(foo-eh-TAY)

whipped

pas de deux

(pah-duh-DOO)

dance for two

penché

(pahn-SHAY)

leaning

pirouette

(peer-oo-ET)

spin

promenade

(prah-meh-NAHD)

walk